# DEAD OR ALIVE

## Short stories

Nathan Tamblyn

Also by the author:

THE MONK'S TALE

LITTLE IDEA

MONKEY KING

To my parents

# Contents

# REPEATED

I am the second incarnation. I am the second incarnation of me. My first life was this one, and its future, but now in the past. This is the second time I have lived this same year.

I will change my future. How could it be otherwise? In my first life, everything was newly learned. But this time I am starting from here, with a life's knowledge and experience. I shall do things differently. Why would I do the same things again? It would be no more satisfying than a repeat viewing. There were moments of great joy and wonder, but they were fresh, and experienced then with a primal urgency. That cannot be recreated. So I shall do things differently. I shall change my future.

Can I change any other future? Will my parents still divorce? Will there still be war in Iraq? Who will win the Grand National? I am not a betting man, or even a horse-racing man, but every man, even a second incarnation, needs money. I cannot survive without food. Or can I? Should I test myself for immortality?

How will I tell my parents?

Maybe I will ask for a guitar.

\*\*\*

Why was I given a second life? Was it given? Or was it merely a chance anomaly of Fate? Did the Dalai Lama know he was reincarnated? Or did the penny only drop when he was told by the search party? He has been reincarnated thirteen times, so he must be getting pretty good at it by now. Doctor Who can only regenerate thirteen times. Is the Dalai Lama on his last turn? Is this second incarnation for me only the start of a series of reincarnations? And if so, will I always be me?

Or perhaps the Dalai Lama just accepted the truth of what he was told. Reincarnation is part of his culture. It is not part of mine. If I went around telling people I was reincarnated, I would be thought crazy. Or ignored. Probably just ignored. Do my parents even understand the idea of reincarnation? Surely they do. Maybe they too are reincarnated! That would make many things much easier. How could I tell? Perhaps I could casually drop it into conversation.

*Thanks for supper, Mum.*

You're welcome.

*I like fish fingers.*

Me too.

*Did you like them in your past life as well?*

What on earth are you talking about?

*Aren't we all reincarnated?*

What? Where did you hear such nonsense?

*Um... playground banter?*

Does someone my age even know the word 'banter'?

\*\*\*

I am six years old. I have been reincarnated as a six-year-old me. What happened to the me that was me before I was six? Where did that me go? But since that was me anyway, perhaps we just merged into one super me. Come to think of it, I have only one set of memories from before I was six.

Or maybe I was reincarnated at birth, and only became aware of this when I reached the grand old age of six. Why that should be, I do not know. But given the unfathomable mystery of why I should be reincarnated at all, it is only a minor perplexity.

I suppose it is better to be reincarnated young and with my life ahead of me, than old and past redemption.

I wonder how old I am really. I remember being thirty-four. That would give me an aggregate age of forty. Maybe I am even older. Perhaps as old as time. If a six year old is asked his age and responds 'as old as time', is that enigmatic and portentous, or just irritating? Would I want people to know how old I am, even if I knew?

What happened to the me that was me in my first life? Did I die? I do not remember dying. Perhaps remembering is not possible. If death is some ethereal off switch to oblivion, then maybe you can only remember up to the point when the power is cut. Descartes said 'I think therefore I am,' I think. So if I am not (because dead), then perhaps I think not, and that would seem to preclude remembering. But then maybe Descartes was wrong.

I do not remember being ill, though. Or doing anything which might have resulted in a sudden death. My last memory was not of driving, or flying, or walking under a ladder. I cannot remember anything to suggest that yesterday was anything other than normal and uneventful. Yet today I am six.

If I didn't die, then what happened to the first me? Am I still there, carrying on as before, routinely unaware that I am also here?

Or did the first me just disappear? Did life carry on for those around me, but without me, an inexplicable disappearance? Do friends and family mourn me, or hope blindly that I might return?

Can I return?

The Dalai Lama never had these problems. He always died before he was reincarnated. Recently he said he might choose to reincarnate before his death. Then there would be two hims. Would the first him lose his memory? Or would both hims share the same memories and then diverge? These are complicated matters for him (or at least the second him). I would not recommend simultaneous rebirth. But then Doctor Who met his former selves several times without undue complications.

But I am the only me here. I am sure of that. This is me as I was. The future me is yet to be. So if I can only be alive one at a time, what happens when this life stops? Will my life continue at a third point in time? Will it revert to my first life? If I die in my second life, if it ends, if it's brought to an end, will I return to my first life?

\*\*\*

Blind panic. Gut-wrenching, bone-shaking, God-fearing panic.

That was my first reaction.

I woke up in bed, and I knew I was awake. Sometimes you can dream you are awake, and it seems real enough. Yet still there is something other-worldly about a dream, even a vivid one, which the unconscious mind can spot if it goes looking for it. Or sometimes a vivid dream is backlit by a mellow softness with a sort of give-away fuzzy quality to the experience.

But my vision had a crisp focus, and there was a bite in the air. My senses were sharp. I was definitely awake.

Imagine you have just remembered that you are supposed to be somewhere important. Maybe a meeting. Or an exam. Or at the airport. Your stomach empties and sinks. A whiff of nausea rises up to your throat. You feel a little faint, you probably look pale, and few beads of sweat trickle down your back. It was that type of panic.

Now multiply that beyond enduring by a gripping terror.

There wasn't any danger. It was not a run-for-the-hills sort of panic. It was the sort that makes you grind your teeth, that makes you tense your fingers into claws and dig them into your thighs. It was the sort that makes you want to cry from the bottom of your soul in the desperate hope that the gods might be so moved by your plight that somehow, who knows how, the misfortune will be reversed.

I screamed and thrashed and scratched and begged until the tears stopped rolling and I crumpled in defeat and exhaustion.

*** 

I must tell my parents. Today, I have discovered, is Saturday. That means on Monday I have to go to school. As a six year old.

Now if I were an eighteen year old, that might be different. Instead of using class to learn things, I could use it to settle scores. Because I now know from the future of my past life that, while my friends are to be cherished, everyone else can shove it. But as a six year old, I have no scores to settle. As a twelve year old, maybe. As a ten year old, even.

(How on earth have these grudges survived more than twenty years and a reincarnation?) But the six year old classroom holds no interest for me. Growing cress hair for an egg-shell face? I think I'm a bit beyond that.

I cannot go to school on Monday. I must tell my parents. I shall ask for a guitar.

*Mum, I would like to play a musical instrument.*

Wow. Where did that come from?

*Could we buy one?*

What instrument do you want to play?

*Classical guitar.*

Why a classical guitar?

*Could we buy it today?*

Today?

*We're not doing anything else, are we?*

Well, no. I will have to talk to your father. Why classical guitar all of a sudden?

*Could you ask Dad? I would really like it.*


A six year old can ignore questions. The conversation of a six year old need not be logical. Not everything he says or does must be rational. Parents come to accept that. I should know. At least, this is true for a four year old. Do parents expect better answers from a six year old? Perhaps parents persist with six-year-old children.


Your mother tells me you want to learn to play the guitar.

*I want to play classical guitar. Can we buy one? I will practice very hard.*

If you really want to learn, I'm sure we can find you a teacher.

*Can we buy one today? Can we go now?*

I wouldn't know what to buy. I think we need a teacher to help us. We can ask at school on Monday.

*The shop can help us. Can we go today? Please?*

What's the rush?

*I can't really explain it. Can we go to the shop to find out?*

\*\*\*

It went like this. We walked into the guitar shop. It was small and badly lit. The windows were grimy. A few shafts of sunlight strained through. Dust particles glinted and swirled. On one side of the shop were classical guitars. On the other, electric guitars. Sounds of a joyless music lesson drifted from the back somewhere. Out front, the shopkeeper wore a grimaced expression of resignation, boredom and aural displeasure. Middle age and lethargy kept him heavy on his stool. Until he noticed us.

Parents! That must mean a sale.

He stood up. A smile stretched his baggy cheeks. He hauled himself an inch taller.

What a delight to see a young gentleman interested in classical guitar – he stressed the word 'classical' with what could only be genuine conviction – and what a discerning choice, because not only is it such a rewarding and beautiful instrument, both in sound and craftsmanship, many handmade by generations of the same family, but in terms of a young gentleman's musical development it is so important to study a polyphonic instrument, for that is the only proper route to a deeper understanding of composition. Now, we have a number of starter guitars – my parents were not especially well dressed, but my father's watch was unmistakeable, and the shop keeper barely missed a beat – but it is important to choose an instrument which is fun to play, so as to encourage practice, and that means a guitar of quality construction and good tone, and it will support improvement through the intermediate grades, while the cheapest ones soon reach their limit, so with an earnest young gentleman a slightly better guitar represents a sound investment, no pun intended, and a longer-term saving.

He needn't have bothered.

'I would like to try the Perez cedar wood guitar please,' I said.

I pointed to a row of guitars on the wall.

His jowls dropped, as if in surprise he had let go of his bags of shopping. Then he remembered himself.

Go with the boy! Let him force the sale!

The guitar was lifted down, and what another discerning choice, and quickly checked for tuning, no doubt a prodigy in the making, and I was ushered towards a stool, such talent must run in the family, and as I touched my fingers to the strings, the flattery fell silent.

The shopkeeper held his breath.

I played *The Coventry Carol*. It uses all six strings and, in the right hand, the thumb and fingers simultaneously. It ends with a surprise Picardy third. It is a simple piece, and very short, at least as I played it. There have been better renditions. But I am only six, my hands are small, and I haven't played it for years, or indeed ever (in this life).

To the shopkeeper, it was the sound of angels.

I thought showing would be an easier first step than telling.

We left the shop with the guitar, and a case, and a footrest, and a music stand, and a metronome, and books of scales and arpeggios and methods and studies and pieces for solo performance.

At home afterwards, there were discussions to be had, mostly between my mother and father. To my great surprise, and greater relief, my own involvement was minimal.

*I have memories from a past life.*

A past life?

*Yes.*

You were a guitar player in a past life?

*I was me. But I also played guitar.*

And you remember that?

*Yes.*

What else do you remember?

*Bits.*

But I remember everything.

***

Blind panic was my first reaction. Because of what I had lost. My wife. My children. My oldest son. My daughter. My youngest son. Aged four and under. My three beautiful babies. Their smiles. Their frowns and pouts. Their arms round my neck. I want to hold them. I want to squeeze them. I want to cuddle up and read a favourite book. I love them. I want to protect them. I want to care for them. I want to give them a home full of love and devoted support, a sanctuary from the world, a castle from which to conquer the world. I want to tuck them in bed safe and happy, and kiss them, and tell them I love them, as I do every night – as I did every night. I want to turn to my wife and smile and hold her close. How

26

lucky I am to have her. How lucky I am to have them – how lucky I was.

*\*\*\**

Time is tight. It will soon be Monday. The guitar has made a point and set the scene. I must now press on and ditch school. This will not be easy. As well as a place to learn, school is also a place to be, and not at home, and parents plan around that. But I shall not be an inconvenience. I need not interfere with my mother's daily routines.

I am quite happy to be left at home alone. Our house was haunted, but we only moved there when I was twelve. Come to think of it though, this house has a side passage between the back and front gardens which was a little spooky. So too the front bedroom. But I am now a most mature six year old, so these things should not be a problem. Anyway, I'll just avoid that side passage.

My mother will resist the threatened loss of autonomy. And both of them will fear for my future without formal education. I shall have to practise my arguments.

Why does the Dalai Lama go to school each time? This is his thirteenth reincarnation. If he can remember what his stick looked like and which pipe he smoked, surely he can remember his maths and scripture.

Perhaps he is a perfectionist.

Perhaps he is still waiting to grow cress hair for an egg-shell face.

Do Buddhists eat eggs?

Doctor Who only went to school once. And unlike the Dalai Lama, and me, he only had one childhood. He grew to be a man, and when he first regenerated he just carried on from where he left off. That is much more sensible. Curiously, he never seemed to age. If anything, he got younger.

What age would I like to be fixed at? Nineteen I suppose. Just for the physical strength and vigour and, looking back, the formidable power of recovery. I suppose I shall know that again.

But I don't want my life to be fixed as it was when I was nineteen. I would miss out on so much that followed. I would never know my children. And I suppose even if my life continued but I remained physically nineteen that too would be problematic. I would be a nineteen-year-old father. However liberal we like to think ourselves, that is still frowned upon. Or met with raised eyebrows. (Eyebrows up, eyebrows down, either way the message the same.) And what would happen once my children reached the same age as me?

I shall have plenty of time for such mental meanderings when I am not at school. I must broach the subject.

*I don't want to go to school on Monday.*

Why not?

*It's childish.*

Hmm.

*It is also a waste of time.*

Why?

*Because I remember it from last time.*

Last time?

*My past life.*

Your past life.

*I remember it.*

You remember what?

*Maths, English, French, everything.*

Everything?

*Oui. Je m'en souviens tout.*

I see.

*Look, if you're worried about certificates, I could have a clutch of GCSEs by the end of next year.*

GCSEs?

*Maybe they're called O-levels. And then A-levels a couple of years later.*

Hmm.

*Would it help if I told you that x squared is two x when differentiated and a third x cubed when integrated?*

Not much.

*There are so many other things I could do with my time.*

Like what?

*Play my guitar for a start.*

You cannot play your guitar all day every day.

*I can play it a lot. And I can read. And write. There are so many books in this world still to be read.*

Hmm.

*Think of the money you'll save in school fees.*

(Thinking.)

You mean you'll never go back to school?

*No need.*

Hmm.

*I might go to university.*

Might you. Which one?

*Cambridge.*

Really.

*Why don't we just take next week off and see how it goes?*

Why don't you just go to school next week and see how it goes?

*Or I could misbehave so badly they kick me out.*

Hmm.


I get next week off school.

I have no magic powers. This is a disappointment. I had hoped that a conscious reincarnation might have so bent the laws of nature in my passage from one life to the next that I might have been dusted with a little cosmic charm. But no. I cannot talk to the animals. I cannot walk through walls. I did try, but I hurt my nose. I thought I might. Perhaps that was the problem. Perhaps nothing less (or more) than full self-belief is called for. I must banish the nagging doubts. And for that, I must wait for my nose to recover.

There is a Buddhist saying: why learn to walk on water when you can use a boat? I was never satisfied with that. Obviously, because walking on water would be awesome. Actually, I have not tried walking on water. Maybe I cannot do walls but I can do water. I shall try tonight. At bath time.

\*\*\*

My parents are trying to understand what has come to pass. They have the gist of it. But what can I tell my sister? I have a little sister. She is four years old. I can hardly tell her that I am a second incarnation. My oldest son and daughter, twins, also four, would not understand. How can I explain to a four year old about the cycle of rebirth?

Is it even a cycle?

It is not as though I have anything to preach. There is no universal law I know to describe. I know only what has happened to me, and even then not much. In fact, here-I-am-again is about the sum of it. What would be the point of telling my sister that? It would be like telling her my middle names. A piece of trivia. Of fleeting interest. She will have questions – all children do – but they won't be about reincarnation. They will be about lunch, or playing outside.

My sister was there at the guitar shop. She saw me play. So what? Her big brother can play guitar. Big brothers can do things, can't they? She has no expectations as to what is possible or normal, and what isn't. That some things are not possible, except that long practice can make them so, for some people at least – an uncertain middle ground between possible and not – that is surely an understanding beyond her experience.

36

If I cannot explain things to myself, and if it is of no consequence to my sister's young life, why say anything at all? But still, what of our relationship? No longer are we separated by a mere eighteen months. And we were close, first rime round. Taken for granted, and these things always are, but close nonetheless, at least as young children. What is to become of our play, our discoveries, our secrets, our mischief?

If I cannot be a father to my children, then I shall be a brother to my sister. I shall not raise her. That is not my station. But I shall give her time – without school, I shall have a surplus of that – and attention and affection. It will not be the same childhood. How could it be? But it shall be close. And for longer perhaps, and with more commitment than the selfish pursuit of my own future previously allowed. No doubt in time there will be questions. But for now they will be of a different order.

*I am not going to school today.*

Why?

*Because I learn better at home.*

Do I have to go?

*Different people learn better in different ways. Anyway, you have your friends at school. It will be good to see your friends.*

\*\*\*

No school means no friends, doesn't it? Last time I was six I had friends. Or at least I had the beginnings

38

of friends. One boy was soon to become my best friend. Another would grow up to be the best man at my wedding. And I at his. And that was just primary school. At secondary school, I would have other friends. They would grow up to be likeable, well-rounded and down-to-earth men, with wives, and children, and happy homes, and careers. And then beyond, friends from university, friends from work. That is all history.

I was never good at maintaining friendships. I was a loyal friend. And good company (sometimes). But this was when life brought me together with other people I liked, in a classroom, in a sports team, in a shared house. When life moved us on, I moved on too, with a new circle of friends. I had few enduring friendships. I had fewer close friendships.

Maybe I should have made more effort. But if truth be told, I am content. Fond memories. I do not cling to them. I can let them go.

But I will need company. I cannot live alone. I tried that once. It was not a success.

So where will a six year old make friends, if not at school? How will a six year old make friends? More to the point, how will a middle-aged six year old make friends? Presumably not with other six year olds. How would we tolerate each other's company? Where would be the common ground? I remember spending a lot of time on my bicycle. But then I grew up and bought a motorbike. I doubt a BMX will hold the same attraction after that.

And how many thirty year olds will want to spend time with me now? Even if they enjoyed my company, how many would feel comfortable? After all, there are registers against that sort of thing.

What about female company?

I remember the first girl I felt for. I was five. She was in another class at school. She had short dark hair. I wanted to hold her hand. It's not as though I am going to track her down. Even in this life, that was a year ago. And it was another country. But the point is, if I have always needed company, then I have always needed female company.

In my first life, it all came together – my limited need for friends, my need for female company – in the form of one woman. My wife. I thought she would be the only person I needed. I vowed fidelity. Till death us do part, we said. Death has not parted us. I am alive. Time has parted us. I might never know what happened to me in my first life, but I am still alive here. The worlds that separate us do not change that. They do not extinguish my vows.

And what if I could return?

I thought she would be the only person I needed. Then we had children. They exhaust my patience. But I need to be there for them. For my children. I need to protect them. I need to share their success. I need to love them. To hold them. To watch them grow strong and independent. To love them still. That they might call and I might not answer. That is a thought which tears me inside.

\*\*\*

It is a curious thing to have the body of a six year old, even if it is mine. I have no hair where previously there was. My skin is soft. My muscles are smooth. I cannot reach as high. I see things that are lower. I am much more bendy.

Dressing myself is an issue. Not because I cannot, but because of my choice. All my clothes have been chosen by my mother. For a six year old. I have not worn corduroy for a quarter of a century. I suppose there is material to salvage. Some plain t-shirts, some plain shorts. But it looks so dated.

And the duvet will have to go. All those spaceships. My tastes are a little different now. I shall raid the linen cupboard (if I can reach). I shall have to talk to my parents.

***

How must my parents feel about this? How would I feel if one of my children told me the same story? Would I feel like I had lost a son? No, I don't think so. He would have the same body, and the same mind tempered by the same memories, but added to.

I think I would feel a desperate need to be useful somehow, to be wanted or needed. My children still depend on me in a multitude of minor ways every day, to help them dress, to prepare food, to reassure them, to comfort them, to read to them, to guide them. And these loving tasks of daily routine are manifestations of a more fundamental dependence, to look after them, to care for them, to love them, to be their father. What comes back is not gratitude but love. Not the love which I have for them. That will never be reciprocated. Reciprocal love is the province of other relationships, of husband and wife. This is something of a different nature. Instead, it is the reassured contentment of being a child, with me as their father. And that means the world to me.

A child's love changes. As my children become strong and independent, they become for themselves less a child and more their own person, a man, a young woman. I wish that for them. But for me, I shall always be their father. And their independence is some way off. I cherish what I have with them now. If that was cut short, if maturity came overnight, unforeseen, unaccustomed, I would feel cheated. I would still need to be needed.

That is how my parents must feel. I can understand it. I can feel it too, but for my own children, and not for my parents. It is hard to get upset for my parents. I am the second incarnation. I am already less the child, and more the man.

***

So the scene is set. But set for what? What am I going to do now? I cannot play guitar all day every day. I have no burning desire to be a professional musician. I thought about it once, in my first life, and although it appealed, aesthetically, the pull was not enough to drive the effort needed for success.

There were things which attracted me in my first life which I had not time for, but perhaps now.

Japanese. Archery. I could start young and train hard. In ten years maybe even become an Olympian!

But for what end? It would have been an end in itself, when I was young, first time, when I had a ferocious appetite for proving myself me, for aspiring to be all that I could, for summoning together everything that I was in a focused moment of extreme demand, to arise the victor, on a higher level of existence, on a par with Nature, breathing the breath of the world itself. But I am older now. I am more mature. I am less impetuous, though occasionally rash. My satisfaction is less hot-headed and energetic, more reflective and subtle.

Movement. There must be movement. Travel too. Because life is in movement, life is a flow. So too my life must flow.

47

How much flow can a six year old achieve? My passport is still attached to my mother's. But had I my own, where would I go? Who would let me in? And I have no money. I am too young to place a bet on the future winner of the Grand National. I do not even recollect the winner until thirteen years hence, assuming he wins again. So am I to be out of money for a decade or more? And even with money, I couldn't go to a pub, or ride a motorbike, not at my age. Can I even go the cinema unaccompanied? And to see what? There are not many films aimed at the mature six-year-old market. I suppose I could sit in a café. Maybe even stay in a guesthouse. Presumably that would be legal. But who would have me?

I was happy to be left alone at home. I am not happy to be housebound.

Housebound doing what? Filling time. Doing things just to be occupied. That's not life, not in any full sense. That only leads to a withering of spirit. True movement, in mind and in body, means progress forward. Above all, it requires creativity. Life is creative. Life is creation.

A father's life can be tedious, full of boring routine and tiresome chores. There is work for the sake of work. But it is underscored by a vital imperative, to support the life of the child, to nurture him or her. It is a powerful instinct and its own reward. It is a participation in the greatest creative activity. It is slow, yes, and exasperating. But it is the nurturing of a life, of life itself in the form of a child, three children, my children. It is challenging and frustrating but an incredible and creative joy.

Where is the joy now? Where is the creativity? My foreseeable future is a decade of filling time. Where is the progress forward in a life repeated? People talk about starting again, but nobody ever does. Fortunes may ebb and flow, but their lives are linear. For better or worse, but always forward. I am trapped in a circle, separated by time from all that matters most to me – from all that matters. What is worthwhile in such a life? Is it a life even worthy of the name?

What would happen if I die? If this second life, less worthy, were brought to an end? Would I return to my first life? Would I be reincarnated elsewhere? Would I still remember? Or would it be the end?

What more do I have to lose?

Is death selfish? My parents would grieve. If it were my child, I would be inconsolable. It does not bear thinking about. I shan't. I fear to entertain even the idea. But that fear concerns my own children. I can understand that my parents would feel the same. But I can only *understand* their loss. I cannot feel it, not when the cause is my own decision, when the loss is me, of my own willing.

And my sister? Can I even understand her sense of loss? Perhaps I can guess what it would be like for me, the adult me from my first life, to lose my adult sister. But how can I understand what it means for a four year old to lose her brother? She calls my name and I do not answer. It is heart-breaking. But the picture in my mind is not her. It is one of my own children, calling out for their lost sibling, and my pain, my reaction, is as their father, wanting to be there to comfort the crying child.

I need to be there. I need to be there more than anywhere, even more than here. Can I cope otherwise? Can I cope without them?

I must talk to my parents.

\*\*\*

*I remember my past life.*

You can play guitar.

*That was a small part of it. But I remember my past life, all of it.*

Since how long?

*Two days ago. I woke up and I was me, but instead of being where I was, I was back here, aged six. My past life was this one. This life is my past one repeated.*

Are you sure it wasn't just a dream?

*These emotions are too real.*

What do you mean?

*I am struggling. I am not sure I can do this again. I am not sure I can start my life again.*

That's a terrible thing to say!

This is a second chance, to do all those things you didn't have time for.

*To do what? As a six year old?*

Whatever you want. We can help. We can make changes. Maybe not all at once. But things don't have to be the same.

You can't have done everything you wanted?

*But I had everything I wanted. A wife. Children.*
*Three children, two boys and a girl.*

(Silence.)

What were their names?

*Even to think about them… I cannot cope without*
*them…*

You can talk to us.

We love you. We can help.

*I don't know what to say.*

What happened to them?

*Nothing. I don't know. I woke up and I was here,*
*without them.*

But with us. We love you. We can help.

*I just want them back.*

Is that possible?

*I don't know. Maybe if I'm not here…*

Don't say it!

(Silence.)

Did you die in your past life?

*I don't know.*

Then death is not the answer here.

*I cannot live without them.*

But you are alive, and we are here, and we can help.

*How can you help?*

You can talk to us. We can support you in every way possible.

We can also get counselling. That might help.

*Counselling?*

You are in grief. You've lost loved ones. This happens to people. It is sad, but it happens.

*How do people cope?*

With friends. With family. With support. You don't have to do this alone.

We love you. Your sister loves you. We can help.

*It hurts so much.*

It will. It takes a long time. And you never forget. But life heals eventually.

And in the meantime, you have us.

\*\*\*

I am the third incarnation. I am the third incarnation of me.

## JUST SO

We all grow old and die, Best Beloved, but it was not always so. It used to be that boys and girls would never age beyond their flowering youth. This was a time before time, if you see what I mean. Time never ravaged, because time never was. How came it to be otherwise?

I heard one mischievous tale from a sour-faced old man, who said that men-folk grew tired from being nagged by women-folk, and so gratefully evolved a progressive deafness followed by a peaceful repose. But he was a lonely old man, as well as sour-faced, no doubt with much to be nagged for, while my own experience of women-folk is quite the opposite, Best Beloved, as well you know.

Then I heard tell from a scientist, of all people, that death was merely Nature's remedy, a necessary solution to the problem of over-crowding, especially at the weekend. Yet when the world was young and wide, there were so few of us, and you couldn't find other people except by shouting, though there's no need to demonstrate. Whereas today, when we do all grow old, well that only seems to have exacerbated the problem of over-crowding somehow. There are more of us now that we die than ever there were when we didn't, if you still see what I mean.

The truth of it all was rather more like this, Best Beloved. Girls and boys had nothing to fear from time, since time was not, as I have explained. So much could be done without threat of interruption.

There was never bed-time. Nor was it ever time to go to school. And so morning stretched into afternoon, only it was all called day, since there was no need to sub-divide it. And day stretched into night, only there was still no need to sub-divide it, so it was all called life. And life stretched on and on and on. How wonderful it might have been for those with an appetite for its wondrous diversity! But that was just the problem, Best Beloved, for after they had sung a little, and done some reading, and helped to put away the laundry, and jumped on the beds, even though they know not to, there were too many boys and girls who began to lose interest. They began to grumble. They became *bored*.

And so it went on. Without imagination, there was nothing to divide up the future. The future was infinite. And the clever thing about infinity is that, even after half way, there is still infinity to go, which is something to do with Maths. The girls and boys got worse, and just lay around, gathering dust, until they had gathered enough dust that they became foothills, and those foothills became mountains, and those mountains became taller.

Up until now, God – though some use a different name – had allowed Nature to take its course, which is really God's course, only slightly less effort and slightly more haphazard. But all this had now gone too far, for God had created boys and girls, and mountains already, so what need was there for more mountains, even if they were tall, especially if there were no girls or boys to draw them? And so God created time, not for anything else, only for people, who immediately complained that they couldn't possibly do everything that needed to be done, even though they had previously done nothing at all, and when nothing was needed anyway, not so far as God could see.

And so it is that people rush around doing ever so much, wearing themselves out, and I suppose earning a peaceful repose after all, when had they the imagination and the patience, they would have grown neither old nor tired. Though I shall never grow tired of you, Best Beloved.

## ZEN FOR AESOP

There was once a panda who lived in the Minshan mountains of China. There used to be thousands of pandas across the whole of southern China and Burma and northern Vietnam. But now only a few hundred lived in the mountains.

He lived alone, but not lonely. He was peaceful. He preferred to avoid confrontation. As a cub, he could climb trees or swim away to escape a snow leopard. But snow leopards were also rare, and he was safe now he had grown up so big. He was almost five feet tall, and weighed twice as much as a man, and three times as much as a snow leopard.

Panda ate bamboo. Nothing but bamboo. He had to eat lots of it, because he was so big. He ate bamboo for breakfast and for lunch and for dinner. Between meals he would snack on bamboo. And whenever he ate, which was most of the time, panda would think. He would think about the weather. He would think about his stomach. But mostly he would think about being a panda.

There were so many things a panda could do. He could climb the mountain. He could have a snooze. He could snack some more. And there were other choices besides. What was the *right* thing for him to do? He never knew the answer. And with that he would sigh, and his heart would ache.

It happened that the bamboo in panda's territory started to die off. This was a natural part of its life cycle. But it was a concern for panda. He needed to find more. Already he yearned for it. So he set off for a walk in the mountains.

There were many other animals that lived in the mountains, and panda would encounter them every day. Some he had seen before. Some were new to him. All of them were kind enough to offer him advice, and he listened thoughtfully.

One time, panda met a sheep called a bharal. It had a silvery coat which shimmered with a pale blue, and thick horns that curved to each side. It was eating the moss which grew between the rocks on the side of the steep mountain slopes.

'You must see the wonder in everything,' it said.

The world was indeed full of wonder. But not everything was wonderful. How could panda see the wonder in an empty stomach? Or in the decay of his forest home?

Another time, panda came across a funny-looking animal called a takin. It had the long nose of a small bison, and the thick coat of a large mountain goat. It was standing on its hind legs, raking its teeth through the leaves on the trees.

'You must laugh at everything,' it said.

Panda liked a good joke. But some days he just didn't feel like laughing. Some days he felt tired or hungry or both.

Yet another time, panda met a bird called a crested ibis. Its bald head was red, its feathers were white, and its long, thin beak was black. It had made its nest at the top of a tall pine.

'I shall teach you rare magic,' it said.

Panda liked magic. At least, he liked watching other people do magic. He might learn how to do it himself, but then what? It was just one more thing he *could* do. He'd be no nearer to learning what he *should* do.

Then one morning, panda saw a monkey. It had a white snub nose and muzzle, but around its eyes was a pale blue. Its shiny coat was deep orange with strands of golden hair. It was wandering the forest canopy, walking on all fours along the branches of the trees.

Panda was by now full of important questions. But every time the monkey replied, it just described the world it saw all around: the warm rays of sunlight filtered through the leaves, the cool puddles of shadow on the ground, the trill sounds and earthy smells of a forest full of life.

And something stirred in panda. It was coming. So the monkey padded off. Panda stood alone. He looked through the trees at the clouds in the sky above him. He thought of the animals he had seen. And then it came.

The world melted away. There were no clouds and no trees. The bird calls dimmed into the distance. He was bathed in an egg of soft light like melted candle wax. Below him seemed to open up a deep chasm. It was black and swirling and full of nothing. His eyes welled with tears. His heart beat in jitters. He resolved to walk on, one foot, then another.

And with that, he heard once again the singing of birds, and the world reappeared as it had always been. He noticed once more the clouds and the trees. The sun warmed his face, and with each breath he savoured the trill sounds and earthy smells of the forest.

And slowly he realized that the nothing he had seen had not been empty. It was infused with life. There was nothing but life. How lucky he was to be alive. He felt this too for the other animals. He felt it for the sky and for the mountains.

After a time, panda found a new place, with more than enough bamboo, for the moment at least. Here too, what was a panda to do? He could climb the mountain. He could have a snooze. He could wonder or laugh or pity his stomach. It was enough, and all there was, just to let life course through him.

And he would start by eating bamboo.


*The purpose of being a panda is to be a panda full of life.*

## MAGNANIMITY

Never was there someone as slow to temper.

Tonight he sat in a restaurant. The place was nothing special. There was a pile of menus on a low table by the door, and he had helped himself to one on the way in. He sat down, just him, at a table for two. The seat opposite was laid with a smeared glass of water and the remnants of a meal from the previous diner. It gave the impression of company temporarily absent. He glanced at the menu, only to settle for the dish he had chosen before coming here, sausages and eggs, but hold the beans. He laid the menu flat on the table to show his readiness. The checked tablecloth was coated in plastic to make it easier to wipe down. That did not appear sufficient incentive to cleaning. But the restaurant was busy. Each table was taken, and most tables were full.

There were two waiting staff, women, each wearing a white shirt and short black apron over a short black skirt. They were rushed about in a graceless way. He watched them each in turn, closely, before choosing the one with blonde hair falling in greasy waves about her shoulders, black roots showing on the crown of her head. She was hassled and frayed. He caught her eye, raising his hand and smiling to draw her in. Of course she saw him. For just a flicker, her eyes grew wide in exasperation. It was another three minutes before she came over.

'Have you chosen?' she said.

He wondered what she might recommend.

She glared through darkening eyes, her head angled pointedly.

He could see she was busy, so just the sausages and eggs, but hold the beans, please.

'Anything to drink?'

No, he was fine, thank you, just the sausages and eggs, but hold the beans.

She marched to the kitchen, all irritation.

He picked up the fork and held it before him. It was a lustreless metal with an oily smudge of fingerprint. He wiped the prongs carefully with a paper napkin. The knife was for cutting; its purpose determined its shape. But the form of the fork spoke of jabbing and piercing. Surely there were other ways of assisting the knife, of getting food from plate to mouth. Yet here was an implement used elsewhere to stab and puncture. He set it back down with a gentle familiarity, and straightened the cutlery to attention. He raised his head and surveyed the room. Over there was an old man, no teeth, slurping hot soup off the edge of his spoon. His pension could afford no finery, and it made his food taste bitter. Over here was a young girl, heavily pregnant, alone, without a ring on any finger, eating toast and jam, and swallowing her resentment. This was a place where tempers could boil over.

The waitress came back. On one side of the plate were sausages and eggs. On the other was a tomato sauce trail of beans scraped back into the pan. As she arrived at the table, he reached across to accept the plate, and knocked over the glass of water.

It splashed across her legs, and lapped over the table into a puddle, splattering her shoes with floor grime.

'You fucking idiot!'

She threw down the plate on the table. The fork bounced once, twice, to fall in a clatter under his chair. The eggs slopped over the side of the plate and some into his lap.

It was all his fault, and he was so sorry, if he might be allowed to help clean up.

'Do whatever you fucking want!'

She stormed off through a door at the back of the restaurant. The room was quiet and all eyes had turned to him, contemptuous and scornful. He brushed the egg off his lap with the paper napkin. He retrieved the fork. He ate what was left of his meal, chewing slowly, eyes shut, feeling the hate grow in

74

the room. When he had finished, he put his knife and fork together neatly upon his plate, and laid the paper napkin over the top. He pulled a black wallet from inside his jacket, and extracted a crisp note, double the price of the meal, and pinned it down with the salt cellar. He stood up, his chair scraping backwards with the sound of fingernails on a chalk board. The soup man swore. The pregnant girl winced. But he smiled apologetically at his fellow guests, and walked with dignity out of the restaurant. Watching through a hatch in the kitchen, the waitress denounced him with a string of muttered obscenities. She took the tip as her due.

It was dark outside. The dull glow of the streetlights sapped the spirit. All they did was reveal the gloom. As he walked along he recalled a story he had once heard told. A gnarly old woman had appeared at the gates of a castle one night asking for food and shelter from the perpetual drizzle. The rich prince looked upon her with disdain and slammed the door shut in her face. But she revealed herself as a witch, with the beauty of a siren to lure men to their deaths, or the haggard features of a crone to drive men to their fate. She cursed the prince to ugly deformity and searing loneliness year upon year. Finally it was love, sealed with a kiss, which delivered the callous prince from that wretched suffering.

He smiled at the happy ending. That night, in the restaurant, the soup man had grown more twisted, the pregnant girl more hateful. He knew that time was running out for their rescue. And as for the waitress, her transformation was complete, nasty and loveless, she had been tempted out one step too far, and the shadows that had fluttered about her heart now cleaved to it. His smile broadened into two rows of white teeth, which parted to let forth a bellow of laughter. He stepped off the pavement and there was an opening, dark and foreboding with flickers of flame. It sucked in the night and the hope, and cast a new shadow upon him, horns on his head, no feet but cloven hooves, a tail that whipped into a point like an arrow head, and red, all red, except those white teeth, still grinning, and dark black eyes, big and round with the maniac joy of another captured soul.

## DEATH

Most people think Death is a white skeleton in a black robe and hood, carrying a scythe. And he is, except that the scythe is for ceremonial occasions only.

Death has never had backache. If Death were to look in a mirror, he would have been able to see his spine, without skin or muscles or anything else in the way to block the view. He would have been able to make any quick adjustment needed to restore his usual perfect alignment. Except that Death has no eyes, only sockets in his skull, and thus has no need of mirrors. And his usual alignment is, as I said, perfect.

If Death had eyes, which he doesn't, he would still have no need for mirrors, because his black robe has a classical simplicity which does not call for elaborate dressing or preening. He had asked for black not, as many believe, so as to reflect the sobriety of his calling, for Death does not consider his duties sombre, but rather because, given his white skeleton, he needed something dark if he was to creep up on people at night. He had asked for a black robe and had been given it. Also, the man in the shop who sold it to him was far too afraid to give Death anything other than what he asked for. Fortunately, that man's idiot assistant was out to lunch, literally as well as figuratively, otherwise Death might have been wandering around in floral patterns.

When people see Death, the usual reaction is panic, screaming, and headless flight, figuratively and occasionally literally. Although such a reaction might be understandable, and certainly Death takes no personal offense, though others before him were quick to temper, it is pointless. Death does not kill anyone. He only collects those who have already died (except once, which was rather embarrassing).*

---

* Death has never been very good with Chinese names. The main problem is the homophones. Once he collected the wrong Chinese person, thanks to a mispronunciation. He soon realized his mistake, because the client was not nearly as dead as he was supposed to be, and Death put him back where he found him the following day, thereby accidentally creating a new religion. Fortunately for Death, that was his only clerical error on record. (These things otherwise make for an uncomfortable time at one's annual appraisal.) As for the cult, it soon disbanded when its leader failed to resurrect any of his followers, mistakenly thinking that his own return must have had something to do with his diet of mackerel.

Headless flights are to be avoided. Death is a practical soul, if indeed he has one, and while the occasional chase might be good exercise, it can take up a lot of time, for dead people do not tire. And on a busy night, the busiest being a full moon in early February, but only in the Northern Hemisphere, there is no time for chase, indeed for anything but escorting the dead to their next destination. Everyone has to be collected. It simply won't do to leave dead people wandering around directionless (and occasionally headless).

Collection itself is a simple matter. Death does not use hand-cuffs. His hand on a shoulder is all that's required. Hence the need for black and creeping: if the first a person knows of Death's presence is his hand on their shoulder, the collection is smoothly done and chasing is avoided. His touch is very reassuring, and dead people want reassurance more than anything else. Death is very good with his hands, which more than makes up for his inability to speak.[+]

Death only works the night-shift (hence again the need for black). There is no day-shift. When people die during the day, they stay where they are, but there is something about the night which releases them. That is when they need collecting. Of course,

---

[+] Death has no vocal chords. But he can whistle. Not by himself, of course, but on a blustery day the wind will sound when it blows through his bones. By moving his arms over his ribs, he can even make out Ode to Joy, though not very well. This is another reason for the robe, not so much for the sake of modesty, because there is nothing indecent about a clean skeleton, and Death is meticulous in his personal hygiene. Rather, it mitigates the possibility of a sudden gust of wind giving away his creeping too early.

day-time here means night-time there, so Death is always on the go, literally too, even though he has no muscles or ligaments. He moves purely by willing it, despite having no brain, and he has excellent proprioception, despite an absence of nerves, all of which gives him an ethereal grace which is forever balletic. And, as I said, dead people do not tire, and Death is dead, indeed he is the embodiment of death, if a skeleton can embody anything. So Death is always as fresh as a daisy (it is others who push them up).

When people die, they are full of questions, and the first person that they come across is Death, if Death is a person, so he has to endure a nightly interrogation, and without even the means of telling them to stop (although, as I said, he is good with his hands). When did I die? How long was I there? Did it smell? What happened to the dog? (Death is only certified to work with humans.) On a slack night, if Death is feeling sociable, he can provide some pretty accurate answers by way of charades. (Did I say he is good with his hands?) But sooner or later the questioning turns along a predictable pattern and ends, as often as not, with the same plaintive inquiry: What is the meaning of life? Nobody ever asks: What is the meaning of death? This might seem tactless, given that the question is always asked of Death, being the embodiment of death, and its guardian, almost too its town crier, if death is a place, which it is. But Death takes no personal offense, though others before him were quick to temper.

At first, Death used to gesticulate a very fulsome answer to the meaning of life. Indeed, it was partly his ability to give a satisfying account of the meaning of life which initially impressed his employers. But although everyone could understand, nobody who did not already know could ever comprehend (and vice versa). So Death adopted a new approach, to save time, of giving a more succinct answer, which was just as accurate, and neither understood nor comprehended any more or less. He would follow this with the wise remark, signed of course, that since they were dead, the meaning of life was now mere trivia, and nothing upon which they could now hope to act anyway. Yet even this obvious reality passed people by without understanding (or, as the case may be, comprehension), so strongly do people persist in clinging to the false importance of past habits. Eventually, in the face of such mass obstinacy, Death simply gave up on providing any explanation at all.

One day, nobody died. This was a miracle, literally, although nobody noticed at the time, not until the hospitals filed their monthly returns, and sought their bonuses for a day of perfect, or at least non-fatal, health care. Of course, the government could not afford to pay out on such a scale, but mostly the hospitals were content to let the matter pass, seeing this was a world-wide phenomenon of unprecedented good luck already. One surgery in Texas did litigate, but only out of principle, because otherwise it would have been the one day that year in which it had neither issued nor been served with proceedings, and so there was its reputation to consider. Its director was also the democratically-elected local representative, and so he settled the litigation by agreeing with himself, all alone in his room, without further need to bother anyone. For this, he was promoted.

The reason nobody died was, as I said, a miracle, literally. Death was unavailable that day. He himself had un-died. He had been born. Perhaps you thought death is the final resting place, and certainly it is restful, except for Death, its embodiment and town crier, who was always kept busy. But it is not final. As every good Hindu knows, even Heaven has a half-life, however long – and it is measured in aeons – but eventually everything must change, and with death the only place to go is life. Death's employers knew this time would come, but chose to make no contingency plans, relying instead on their omnipotence. But on the day of Death's un-death, there was a complicated catastrophe unfolding in another realm of existence which was simply too interesting to ignore. Unable to devote the time which finding a replacement for such an important job really demanded, instead they activated the miracle of nobody dying.

Nobody died, but one extra person was born, Death, although nobody noticed, not even when the hospitals filed their monthly returns. And of course his parents gave him a different name. Really, Death was less of a name, and more of a title, attached to a job which he no longer had, and did not remember anyway, which was just as well, since what he had seen, were it a film, would have been certified only for a person much older.

Naturally, a replacement was found, and Death looked very fine on the day of his inauguration, a gleaming white skeleton in a pristine black robe and hood, carrying a scythe (this was, after all, his ceremonial investiture).

He too never had backache.

## OUTSIDE

Tuesday

Noisy day. Others caught wind of a new-comer. No chance of being left alone. They want my opinion. Not to heed it. Only to prolong the discussion.

Thursday

Quieter. The weather is changing. Less heat means less agitation.

Friday

Same food. Never any choice. But today there is fruit. Eat mine quickly. Turn your back, and it disappears.

Monday

Glimpse visitors. None for me.


Tuesday

Another week. Nothing new. Except the weather. There's a breeze in the leaves. Cannot see the clouds. No sky from here.


Wednesday

Woken for cleaning. Moved into next room. Others make a big show about it. Suppose it breaks the routine. Watch the floor get mopped. Cleaner tries to ignore the fuss. I wonder.

Saturday

Early morning. Walk around the perimeter. One lap only. Drag it out. Others slump in the corner. But I still remember. At least I think I do. Patches of sunlight pull me away.


Monday

Another apple. Bruised. Toss it away in disgust. Nearly cause a riot. Any excuse will do. Someone eats it.


Tuesday

Time. Too much of it. A few faces come and go. One interesting. None interested.

Friday

Summer has definitely passed. Now the wind blows
through. Nights a little too long. Soon there won't be
enough patches of sun to go around in the mornings.
Another winter. And me still here.


Wednesday

Cleaning day. Already awake. Moved into next room.
Others make a big show about it. Watch the floor get
mopped. Cleaner tries to ignore the fuss. Always the
same routine. I wonder.


Thursday

I plan. Others don't remember. I do. I can still taste it.
Inside is stifling. Outside the pulse quickens. And so
will mine.

Saturday

Waiting. Impatient. Agitated. Others sense a difference. Teasing. A fight. But nothing lasts in here. Confinement breeds lethargy. It's probably in the water too. We all believe the myths. They're the best stories we've got.


Monday

When did I last wash? Next time it rains, I'll put my hands through. Maybe even drink a little.


Tuesday

Tuesday forever.

Wednesday

Cleaning day. Moved into next room. Watch the floor get mopped. Always the same routine. Others make a big show about it. Cleaner tries to ignore the fuss. Ignores too well. I make a break for the door. Not subtle, but speed makes up for that. Others go crazy. Glad for the noise; muffles the shouts of alarm. Reckon to have about ninety seconds head-start. Second door left open. Through it, and outside in the yard. The air tastes different already. Colder and fresher. Race for the wall and scramble up. Pause on top to look back. Others whoop and cheer – or jeer, but not at me. Jump into bushes. Lurch onto the pavement. How big is this world outside! Startle two people. They point in panic. Everyone here is treacherous. A side door opens. How could they muster so quickly? I hear shouting. Dart across the road and under a parked car. Catch my breath. One chance left. Gather myself. Shuffle out, and off like a sprinter. A shot. My leg stings. I keep going. Maybe ten seconds. Then black.

Monday

Awake. Back inside. No chance of being left alone. Others inquisitive. Glad for the company.

Thursday

Same food. Get an apple today. Eat mine quickly. More visitors than usual.

Friday

Walk around the perimeter. One lap only. Others slump in a huddle. Weather is cooling.


Wednesday

Cleaning day. Others make a big show about it. Suppose it breaks the routine. Watch the floor get mopped. They don't remember the outside, but I do. At least I think I do. Cleaner tries to ignore the fuss. Always the same. But the door's open. I wonder.


*Dedicated to the buff-cheeked gibbon, formerly, and then latterly, of Hong Kong zoo, 5 October 2011*

## FLOWER

Tonight was the party to mark her final days at university. She kept her body shielded by the shower curtain against the first blasts of cold water as her hand reached through to turn on the tap. The sound of gushing air and a faint rattle of pipes warned it was coming. Quickly she pulled back to safety. Once the steam began to rise, she stepped into the porcelain basin and a half room of white tiles with a small frosted window. It was barely ajar. Although she could have watched those passing below, she herself was nude and unseen. The shower head was a flat metal sieve in the middle of the ceiling. She stood underneath as the water rained down like a summer storm. Her hair was darker now in the wet, and she parted it from her face, smoothing it back as it clung close to her head and neck. Drips ran in tracks down her body. She closed her eyes to follow the streams as they explored new angles. She washed in a sparse lather of orange blossom. Her hands roamed over her breasts, and under, cupping each in her palms. Then she slid down the curves of her sides and hips. Her right hand glided over her stomach, while her left ventured further, over her pubis to a small patch of wet hair. Her middle and forefinger moved in between, teasing the soft folds. She bent lower to wash her legs, one at a time, the gushing water splashing off her lower back, both hands rubbing in circles from high on the inside to all the way down.

Back in her room, she put on some music, something light and up-beat, a female singer. She let drop her towels and pulled up some knickers, black and wispy. As the chorus came round she stopped to join in. She sang along in a summery voice with glints of anticipation. She raised her arms above her head as her hair fell in tresses about her cheeks. Her hips wiggled in echo of a dance, her bare breasts in a gentle bounce. As the song faded she turned to the mirror. She pouted her lips to apply some colour, pink in a soft hue. She pressed together the pads of her lips and sucked them into a pop. She giggled. Then on to her eyelashes, and this time some black, her mouth falling open, her tongue arching upwards, frozen still in concentration. She blinked and blew a teasing kiss before turning from the glass.

The wardrobe revealed a small but selective array of dresses in pinks and flowers. She pulled out two, draping each in turn over her body before casting one to the floor beside. The other she lifted above her head and it fell in ripples of soft cotton over her skin. The shoes followed naturally, bright and shining, with a pointed heel, but a low one. She tapped out a rhythm on the wooden floor that brought out a smile which was kind and disarming. She switched off her light and closed the door behind her. She skipped down the corridor, her dress floating about her thighs. From out of sight two squeals of delight mingled and drifted as friends grasped hands.

She was happy and playful and creative and strident and loved and desired and wanted. What did it matter that her birth certificate once said she was a boy?

## THE RED PLANET

It had been two hundred days in the rocket. To his surprise, he had grown fragile with loneliness. He was cut off from conversation and companionship, and not only people, but from the clouds and the rain and the ripples upon a calm sea. There was nothing here in this sterile solitude of metal and wiring to nourish his mind or soul. Something in him was dying with each mile further into the empty abyss of infinite space and away from the planet which had born and nurtured him. The recycled air in the capsule was sour with grief and mourning.

\*\*\*

The metal clattered and juddered, and he with it. He had lost his physical resilience. Of course he had done his exercises: two hours each day on the treadmill and the resistance machines. But so long without the weight of gravity bearing down, what had once been rugged was now yielding. The passage through space had been smooth as ice, and his body had been lulled, grown malleable with the ease. Now as he entered the atmosphere of Mars, the mounting waves of pressure shook ripples through his innards. The bolts around him strained and scratched as the steel groaned, the rocket wrung and stretched as it fought to maintain its bearing, little more than rivets and metal sheets against the brooding mass of a planet.

He could now see land, if that was the right word for it, and he strained to reach the lever in front of him. He pulled with effort, both hands, sweat prickling on his back. He frowned hard as if the exertion would empower his arms. The vibrations reverberated in his teeth, and his eyes bulged. The rocket swooped in one final turn, nose to the sky, as the blast engines, with the last of their fuel, fired underneath to slow the descent. A thuddering impact threw up clouds of dust and one last jolt. He found himself breathing hard, still clutching the lever. He released his grip. He held a long breath. The revolving whine of the engines slowed to a halt and the metal settled down into stillness. Then all he could hear was a whistling wind which rose and fell in eerie tones upon the barren plains before him.

\*\*\*

One more year. One more year, second by second, minute by minute, until the next crew arrived and he wasn't alone. He had to signal the all-clear, and then one more year. He had lasted longer than that in the test confinement back at base. But that was on Earth. The sun was closer. The rotation under feet was natural and familiar. There were trees and birds beyond those walls, and beyond the door, people, if he needed them. But here, on this red planet, in wild and desolate isolation, his mind was narrow with a fearful regret, a restless paranoia which gnawed away at his strength and sanity.

*\*\*\**

He dropped from the ladder onto the parched soil. His suit made movement awkward and slow. Inside his helmet, the air grew humid, and his visor began to mist. Each breath filled his ears. Every pulse of heartbeat throbbed in his brain. He raised up both arms, then accelerated them down, the javelin point of the flag-mast piercing through the cracked ground. Immediately he feared this impertinence. He felt a weight upon his back. He turned in a clumsy slow motion, his mind in jitters, eyes growing wide, the colour fading from his face. But there was nothing to see. No canals or tracks or vegetation. He was alone, two hundred and thirty days, fifty million miles from the nearest person. His eyes closed, a moment of defeat, but at once he opened them, casting about in panic, straining to see in the landscape the single change that would betray a presence. The adrenalin coursed like a flash flood through muscles tight and brittle.

Follow the protocol. One foot at a time, each following the other. Forward, over the crumbling stones. Down, past a slope of collapsing shale. Round, behind that outcrop, chipped and disintegrating with each howl of the passing wind. Everything here was collapse. The planet was inhabitable only as a rock underfoot. This was no crucible of vitality, merely an object, floating in space, upon which to stack containers of life orphaned from another world. Here he was, alien to this place, alive upon a dead planet, and himself cut off, struggling, dwindling. There was no leaving. That wasn't the plan and there wasn't any fuel. He was the first of a vanguard, a new colony. But no man could hope to survive here, in this place of persistent and timeless decay.

He looked back at the rocket. Already its legs had sunk deeper into the dirt. Its underbelly was stained red with a fine silt that was creeping upwards, eating into a metal which was flaking away in steel ash. The wind blew in gusts and whines. His skin felt shrivelled. He must get back inside. There was safety in that metal can. He could bolt the door against this bare desert. The walls would close in around him.

Out here he was exposed, the empty unknown expanding in all directions, each swirl of dust the hinted presence of some unseen danger. He was breathing too hard and his eyes were sore and dry with staring. His mind struggled against the madness of his presence on this tortured carcass of a planet. What could ever live here?

Each laboured step brought him closer to the rocket, to safety, to the total collapse of his nerves as his heart beat faster and the sweat poured. His eyes saw in glimpses and flashes. His ears heard in thumps and shrieks. The wind whipped and the rocks flaked and the shingle fragmented into plumes of red powder, and everywhere a lurking peril. One hand now on the ladder. One hand on the wheel that would turn to open the door.

But it rose up behind him like a shadow grown long at dusk. It moved with abandon, consumed with fear, and turning over upon itself. It rode upon a wave of menace to the echo of wailing and anguish. And it was coming with all the doom of inevitability.

He shook with terror, his back to the waste sands, not daring to look behind. He sobbed as he gripped the door, his knuckles white, each quarter turn of the wheel rusty and scraping. Two more turns. The dust was billowing. One more turn. The wind lashed about in screeches. And it bore down upon him, black and oppressive and crushing the life from him. The door swung open, and he fell inside, dead.

As the soil gathered about the craft, back on Earth they were celebrating, glittering lights and excitement in an evening summer garden, a party to mark the landing. Amid fluttering moths and the chirp of insects, they told each other stories about the thrill of adventure. And they went home, late, well fed from a night of good cheer and company.

## SCARS

Newburgh is a place where violence is ugly. Some speak of a curse upon the town. Others call it a blessing. It's a place where violence results in a scar – upon the face of the aggressor.

Children are not exempt from these consequences. And children fight all too often. But young children also have bodies which heal overnight, and which grow, replenishing and adding to what was there. Any scars suffered as young children might become imperceptible with time, or perhaps disappear altogether. But as a person ages, the ability to heal diminishes. It's a bit like moods: children can scream blue murder one moment, and the next it is all forgotten with a new game; but adults bear grudges. In Newburgh, the taller the person, the more likely the scar will last. 'You are old enough to know better,' they say.

The town has its fair share of rough and tumble. To shouts of delight, fathers throw their children about in the swimming pool. To cheers of encouragement, football players launch themselves into tackles on the pitch. In cinema lines on a Saturday night, teenagers jostle and shove as they tease about girlfriends. But a mind tainted by anger is something else. Spite turns contact into violence.

Martin had no scars. He had wrinkles which attested to the worries of parenthood. A few white hairs provided corroboration. But otherwise his face showed with a tired but patient understanding. He slept well what nights he could. He went for walks

114

when solitude was necessary. He took the trouble to listen to people and respond with dignity. He had friends, but not too many. He had a job, and it wasn't all bad. He was a loving father and a peaceful man who sought virtue for his own health and as a model to his children.

One evening in July, Martin was walking home with his son. He had been to the school to listen to the choir. The performance had ended. He had applauded with honesty. They were now only the distance of a short conversation from the supper awaiting them on the kitchen table. Advancing up the pavement was another man. His shoulders were slumped and his head bowed. He walked with bravado and intent. Under each approaching street lamp, the scars on his face showed up. Some looked white and settled. One was raw red. Martin stepped to the side to let the man pass, and called his son out of the way. But his son was too young; it takes time for any urgency to sink through the layers of distraction in the mind of a child who is staying up late and chattering away. The boy heard too slowly. He tried to skip out of the way, but was only more in it. In the collision, the man lost his stride, and the boy was bowled to the rough concrete. Martin turned to his son who was grazed and tearful. But the other man felt an insult more pressing than the needs of an injured child.

The man demanded an apology and was given one. But his bile was flowing and his muscles too primed to be satisfied so mildly. He loomed up close to Martin, leaning in, spitting his words with a taste for anger, his eyes big with a nasty pleasure. The boy's face went pale and long with fear, and his crying took on notes which were small and plaintive. Martin asked please could he help his son, but the man only grew in agitation and disgust. He shoved with two hands, stepping forward to tower above Martin, who stumbled to the ground. Martin stretched out a hand to cushion his fall, but the jolt of it ran up his arm and jarred his shoulder. The pavement scraped away on his palm, white flaps of skin beside bloody grooves flecked with grit. He tripped over himself to get back on his feet, his son now wailing in the forlorn misery of watching his father so dominated and oppressed.

Martin heard the cries, and the sound rang sharp in his ears. It quivered his body. A flush of indignation fired him to throw out a punch, his first ever, and so unexpected that the other man was still stepping forward onto it. Fist struck head. Dunk. And when the momentary mist of blackout had lifted, the other man discovered such searing agony in a dislocated jaw that he staggered off, tilting to the left, and clutching his face. Martin ran to his son who sat silent and stunned, open-mouthed, eyes blank in the shock of victory. Martin lifted him up, and the child threw both arms tight around his father's neck, head buried deep in Martin's shoulder. Martin squeezed him closer, reassuring him with a gentle stream of loving words.

After a while, the boy leant back. He was calmer now. He looked with a tender curiosity upon his father's face. There on the cheek was a small red

118

line, not a wrinkle, but something more like a cut freshly closed. He reached out a small hand to feel the skin, and with one little finger traced the line of the scar. He had pride and admiration in touching the wound. And that was enough for the tiniest scratch to appear on the baby-soft skin of that boy's beautiful face. 'Sins of the fathers,' they say in Newburgh. And the tears began to pool in Martin's eyes.

## SPRING HOUSE

Some houses have character. Some houses can harm. When I was twelve, we moved to a new house. It was on a gated estate which consisted of two main roads, one flowing off the other, and a number of smaller tributary cul-de-sacs. There was a golf course running up the hill and across the estate, and a deer park at one end. Altogether it was rather upmarket. Our new house was down a leafy lane wide enough for one car at a time. The other houses there hid behind hedges and trees. This was a road which spoke of seclusion rather than neighbourliness. Ours was at the end, and since we moved there in May, my mother named it Spring House. It was set back from the road, in the middle of its garden plot, a carriage driveway sweeping up to the house and then out again. It was a double-fronted brick house with large bay windows, and steps leading up to a pillared porch and the front door. Though no-one had cause to pass this way, still the house was veiled behind a dense hedge of high laurel. There were old oak trees and silver birches in the garden, but they later blew down in an October storm, nearly flattening the house. That week, the whole estate was transformed into an unfamiliar jungle of trunks and branches and foliage through which my sister and I clambered and explored.

My bedroom was at the front of the house. It looked out over the carriage driveway and a cherry blossom tree whose naked branches in the winter moonlight would throw puppet shadows on the wall by my cupboard. There was a landing, three sides of a square, with my bedroom at the start, next to the stairs which led down and round into the hall below. Across the landing was my sister's bedroom, smaller than mine, but she was younger than me. My parent's bedroom was the last corner of the square, at the back of the house, the far end of the landing. On the wall outside their room hung antique guns that my father had cause to acquire in his adventures overseas as a young man. Standing in my bedroom door, I could look down, past the stairs, diagonally across the hall, and through into the kitchen. Beyond the kitchen used to be an outdoor patio with a high wall and a metal gate. What sinister need there was to lock away one part of outdoors from another I never knew. But a roof was put upon that high wall,

122

and the gate replaced with a door, and so it became our playroom.

Children take fright easily. Perhaps this is thanks to an imagination not yet tempered by experience. Perhaps children are more attuned to what adults with their mundane burdens have no time to heed. But there was something wrong with Spring House. A brooding darkness would visit. There were days when I could feel it in the playroom. It should have been a pleasant thing, for the view and the air, to have open that door which led to the garden. And yet opening it seemed to me a risky invitation. Part of me wanted it unlocked anyway as an escape route, why and from what I could not tell. But the larger part of me knew that any way out was also a way in. Even when the heaviness was already inside, still I sensed that there was more to come if only given the opportunity. Those were not moments to be alone, but in company, and preferably elsewhere.

I cannot say when the physical emanations started, but I do know where: in my sister's bedroom. She had a small cupboard in one wall and the recurrent fear of a creature sequestered behind her clothes. But there was no flight of fancy about her bedroom light. It was a white orb which hung down from the middle of the ceiling. And sometimes it would start to swing. Even when the window was closed, and the bedroom door was closed, and there wasn't a breath of wind the length of the county, still it would swing, oscillating like a pendulum for divining. This was a small phenomenon, nothing big enough to be definitive or send for the vicar, too trifling to be accorded the attention of rational adult minds, but too deliberate and insistent to be ignored by a child when alone in the room in the dark. So too it's the small noises trying not to be heard which cause the most fear.

And it was noises which came next. On my own in the bedroom, footsteps would fall upon the stairs, climbing up from the hall – and my room the first any ascending visitor would come across. There were never enough footfalls to account for the entire flight. The climb would stop a few stairs short of the top, as if the person, or whatever it might have been, was waiting, biding their time until I came through my bedroom door. Then after a while the process would repeat, beginning somewhere near the bottom, a slow and rhythmic pace, dom, dom, dom, the muffled sound of foot on carpet, about the weight of a man. Quite independently, my sister had such terrors about something coming up the stairs that she was moved further round the landing to another room at the back nearer to our parents. That did not stop the noises, which were added to, the sound of a kettle boiling, or a teaspoon rattling in a cup, even though the kitchen was empty.

Perplexity can inspire curiosity. But for me it was just fright. It came to a head one afternoon when my mother went out to collect my sister from school. I was left to myself. I had spent the day at home with a sickness. Playing in my bedroom, I heard again the steps on the stairs, and again they stopped near the top, just outside my bedroom door, just behind the wall. And then the breathing began. It was not my own breathing, since I was near paralyzed with fear, not daring to move, not risking even a whisper of sound to give away my location. I felt that the smallest change would give the excuse for that catcher waiting outside to pounce and terrify. And the breathing continued. Not heavy panting, but slow and controlled, deep breaths through the mouth, waiting breaths, ready breaths, not trying to be disguised or hidden, prepared to be noticed. For an eternity I sat on the floor, staring at the open doorway, frozen in motion, unwilling to chance even raising a thought. Then finally, whether it was courage or madness, I grabbed for a racket under my bed, and letting out a frenzied war cry, I charged through the door, racket swinging in flailing arms.

There was nothing on the landing, so I ran around to grab a gun off the wall. Shouting warnings for all to hear, I chambered the barrel as if loading it to shoot. It was decommissioned, but in my fiery craze I supposed that I alone would know that for sure. I bundled through each room in the house, behind every door, in every cupboard, screeching my attack, jabbing at clothes and curtains with the muzzle of my rifle, until, having ransacked the whole house, I went out through the front door and sat in the middle of the street, staring back at the windows, watching obsessively for any movement. And that was where my mother found me upon her return.

I escaped to boarding school, or so I thought, and so too my sister a year or so later. In our absence our parents filed for divorce. Perhaps it was written.

More likely to me the evil which clouded the house had found another outlet. Unable to brutalize the children, it had infected the adults. And what it gave out it got back. We couldn't sell the house at first, so there we all were, divorcing parents, and children back during vacation, all under one roof, angry and loathing and miserable, charging up the bricks with malice for the next occupants. We did sell eventually, but just before then we received a letter to the previous owners. Having nowhere to forward the letter, my parents opened it. It came from a place called the Black Rose Clinic, a final invoice for the inmate care of a child now dead, sent to an address which no-one had sought to update.

Perhaps I have been unfair. Perhaps it was not the house at all. For I have one final night to tell of, and that happened to me at school. My boarding house was a solid construction of steel and concrete and cold war paranoia. There was a bomb shelter in the basement, and the corridor curved to inhibit any blast wave travelling straight from one end to the other. It also precluded a direct line of sight. My small room was at one end, on the ground floor, looking out to the side upon a paved path which drew out the boys from their houses to the school rooms. The windows had restraining bolts so that they only opened part way, not enough for anyone to get in, or more likely, for anyone to get out in the first place. At any rate, the windows were shut that night, and my bedroom door, like every other, was shut too. It was late evening in autumn. I had finished my work and got into bed. The light in my room was switched off. There was a street lamp outside the window which cast a mournful orange glow. It seeped through the curtains and into the room, but that didn't stop me from falling asleep.

Then at once I was awake, an imprecise midnight. The room was pitch black, impossibly so, and I lay there in bed, horrified, isolated in the midst of a darkness which seemed infinite. And there at the end of my bed, unseen, was pure evil, menacing and gloating and looming over me. I was unable to move, and unwilling even to breathe for fear that this might acknowledge my waking and so cause the visitor to engage me. Sweat blistered on my brow, and my heart beat in panicked palpitations, too loudly. Then exhaustion pulled me back to oblivion. But I awoke a second time. Twice that night I was visited. Twice

I collapsed back into unconsciousness. In the morning, the world was the same as it had been. A warm sun shone through the curtains to bathe the room with reassurance. I had been tested. I had survived.

## HESPERIDES

He was born immortal, but not quite. A bite from an apple of the tree of the Hesperides could kill him. This he knew, as he knew many things, for his earliest memory was knowing everything that everyone else already knew, and other things besides. Not for him the gradual accumulation of knowledge. There was only one thing he wanted: to take a bite from an apple of the tree of the Hesperides. This would kill him, as he knew, but he wanted it all the same.

Often he ate apples. He was not afraid of being poisoned. Only an immortal could find the tree of the Hesperides, let alone succeed in taking an apple from it. And since the immortal would want the apple herself, she would never waste it poisoning another. That was his thinking, anyway. For all he knew, and he knew all, he was the only immortal. Or perhaps he ate apples because he enjoyed the frisson in these isolated moments of risk.

Because there were no other risks in his life. Some people climbed mountains. Some dived down to the depths of the ocean. These were great feats, except for an immortal. He could scale heights and plumb depths with little effort. Not that he was impervious to nature; he could still be blown off or washed out. But there was no lasting consequence. Some people climbed mountains. The effort and the giddy heights were an exciting distraction. For an immortal, they were the mundane reality. Some people climbed mountains. Of course, they came back down again. But soon enough they would be casting around for the next ascent, the next distraction. Up or down, to him it made no difference. Wherever he went, there he was.

His greatest challenge was life itself, having to face up to the ordinary, without the illusion of transient thrills to provide any escape or relief. But at least he was alone, without weakness, and with none to bind him. He had met hermit monks who spoke of the privations of their existence, the cold winters and the rumbling bellies. Does martyrdom count if it comes at one's own hands? And anyway, these monks were free beyond measure. They too were unbound from the shackles of responsibility. For he had also met fathers, and seen with his own eyes the tight restraint of paternal duty. The shared affection of father and son was the very bond of love which tied down the man.

With nothing to learn and without adventure, he found no common cause to share with others. He was walking a path where everything was monochrome, including the people who came across it.

He did not have to eat. He was immortal, so what did he care for calories? He did not have to eat, except for an apple from the tree of the Hesperides. In this he had no choice. There was a nausea churning in the pit of his stomach which drove him ever onwards, towards that garden. Day after day he sought it out. The seasons revolved and he barely noticed. Year after year, but what was time to an immortal? Death after death, but not his own, and he had no-one to mourn. Step after step he drew closer. And after all eternity he was finally there, the garden at the end of the world.

Plants had reclaimed a crumbling perimeter wall, knotting themselves into a more discrete and impenetrable barrier. Iron gates rusted quietly. According to the oldest stories, the garden was kept by nymphs, and protected by a dragon which never slept. But when he arrived, he found only a man, a mirror image of himself, and the way was barred. So battle was joined, an act of violence, to free the way to pluck an apple, an act of violence, to receive from its poison the constriction of death, an act of violence. Except that the fight never happened. He knew he would win, as he knew everything, and that knowledge was enough to make it so.

137

Now he held the apple. He felt the menace of its weight. He saw its long shadow. He traced a finger over the golden orange of its smooth skin. He raised it to his nose. Its scent was of evening dew and falling blossom. He bit into it. It crunched like thunder in his head, and released a tang which was sugar sweet and potent like cider. He could soon be drunk, but not in this life. The juices trickled down his tightening throat, and just as he swallowed he thought to himself:

'Ah, so this is fear.'

## DAISY

Daisy was a cow. And she was pregnant. This was her second child. Winter was cold, but the baby inside kept her warm. The day when he first kicked – she was convinced it was a boy – brought her a joy she hadn't known for many months. As spring approached she grew progressively wearier, but she radiated a sense of happy purpose. She was a natural mother.

Now she was in labour. The early contractions were a severe cramp, but there was time enough between them to get excited by the news they brought. Soon though the contractions came long and almost continuously. At first the pain was immense, and she lowed in agony, and although that never subsided, eventually exhaustion meant her mind sank, immersed and resigned. A kindly man was attending to her. He stroked her flanks and said soft words she couldn't understand but which sounded like praise. And with the passage of hours the child's head emerged. There was a final push which twisted and tore in a torment so excruciating her voice tore apart the night and she feared the worst. But the child dropped, squashed and bloody and alive, onto the hay beneath her. It was a boy.

Spent beyond measure, she turned to the new one. Her eyes were sleepy but their embers glowed with love and pride. She licked her son gently, cleaning away the trauma of his birth, nuzzling his face. And after a while his lips reached for her teat, pulling back to the roof of his mouth as her milk flowed, nourishing and life-giving. The kindly man patted her and stepped away. Forward from the shadows came another. He yanked at the child and pulled him away, leading him from the stall. She turned to follow, confused and afraid. The gate was shut. The child was dragged from sight. Not again. Not a second time. And she lowed in a wail that ripped at her soul, her heart thudding madly with terror and despair. And she lowed in a wail that tore through her sanity, her guts tied in knots and her mind delirious. And she lowed in a wail that lasted a lifetime.

Her milk was bottled and destined for others.

## OBITUARY

Winston Churchill, who has died aged fifty-seven, was best known as a conspicuous consumer of expensive food, having won the largest lottery jackpot in history. He only ever bought one ticket. He was a short man, and the tabloid media found great excitement in charting his progress from whippet thin to near perfect sphere. He himself never cared for their opinions.

His first act as a multi-millionaire was to hire the Coliseum in Rome for a private dinner function. He invited every music star whose album he had bought as a child. Pizza was served by young men dressed as gladiators. Champagne was poured by young women dressed as nymphs. After that, he dedicated himself without respite to the finest education of the palette that money could buy. His goal was to endure the private cooking of every chef recognized with a Michelin star. This quest would take him around the world, and he liked to boast of more foreign travel than the US Secretary of State. He flew in a private plane, painted yellow, 'my favourite flavour of Angel Delight.'

Winston Dudley Churchill was born at home in Bolton. His father was a bricklayer and his mother a seamstress. His childhood was frugal. He left school at fourteen to train as a plumber, helping to support the family when his father was unable to work because of Alzheimer's. Winston never left home, but continued to reside with his mother in their terraced house even after the lottery win. The

143

only home improvement he made was the purchase of a microwave oven.

\*\*\*

William Shakespeare, who has died aged two, was the first human clone. He died with his mother in a house fire. The cause of the fire has not yet been established.

His parents met at university, where they were both studying biological sciences. Subsequently they became leading researchers into genetically inherited diseases. William's father contracted a virulent cancer while still young. The decision was taken to freeze the father's sperm before chemotherapy. The father died six months later. His widow then discovered that she was infertile. She campaigned for many years for the right to clone a child from her husband's sperm. Eventually Parliament was persuaded of the medical value in such pioneering science, and passed legislation which allowed human cloning in certain limited circumstances.

William Hector Shakespeare was born in London. There were scenes of angry demonstration outside the hospital. The ward was emptied for William and his mother alone, and police guards were stationed outside around the clock. Despite tales of doom foretold in the media, William was born a healthy child. He received extensive medical examinations every three months, and doctors described him as playful and good-natured.

William's mother wrote a popular book about her experiences. She retired on the royalties, and hoped to live quietly with her son out of the limelight. The family burial site has been kept secret.

*\*\*\**

Joanna 'Blind Jo' Lumley, who has died aged eighty-nine, was a blues harmonica player. She wasn't blind. That was a family joke when, as a child, she walked into a plate glass door on her first visit to a supermarket. But the name stuck. Even her teachers at primary school started using the moniker.

Joanna Magdalene Lumley was born in Detroit. Her father was a preacher, and she used to sing with her mother in the church choir. She was a wayward child who would climb out of her bedroom window at night and hitch-hike into town to visit dance halls. She smoke and drank, which often prompted a belting from her father.

Her parents were killed when shot during a robbery. They were locking up the church office one night when a group of youths burst in. Jo was next door and heard the shots and screams. By the time she had hurried to the room, the attackers had already fled, but she never forgot what she saw. 'It's there before my eyes every night I play,' she once said.

The death of her parents shook her badly, and she wandered the streets for six months. One passer-by donated a harmonica instead of money, and she began to play. Soon she was earning enough money from busking to pay for a hostel room. She landed a job as a backing singer at a local club until the owner heard her playing the harmonica in the dressing room. She was given her own slot that very night. News of her talent soon spread. She is the only musician to have played at the inauguration of a US President and the coronation of a King.

\*\*\*

Peter Sellers, who has died aged ninety, was a military enthusiast who enjoyed re-enacting famous battles from English history. On one early occasion, he was invited to Mississippi to participate in a re-enactment of the American civil war, but he found the participants' use of modern English dialogue so

148

distracting that he vowed thenceforth only ever to die on English soil.

Peter Harry William Sellers was born in Darlington, the eldest of six sons. His mother and father worked in an automobile factory, and he was later apprenticed there. He continued to work there during the Second World War, when the factory was converted to producing munitions. His skills were an essential contribution to the war effort, but he regretted being unable to fight at the front with his brothers. Four of them died in battle. After the war, he worked in a fireworks factory until retirement.

His favourite battle was Hastings, which he re-enacted more than one hundred times. He was always on the losing side. He played King Harold only once. His attention to detail was legendary among fellow enthusiasts, and his wife resigned herself to a week of him living in character before every fight. He amassed a considerable range of costumes. Many of these contained authentic details scoured from car boot sales or internet auction sites. They are now housed in a new display at the Imperial War Museum.

***

Paul McCartney, who has died aged seventy-two, was Britain's most convicted criminal. He put his success down to petty crimes. 'Serious crimes mean long prison terms,' he once said, 'and less time for reoffending.'

His early specialism was offences of being drunk and disorderly on railway lines, which as a teenager he managed to double up with convictions for underage drinking. A health scare with his liver led him to becoming tee-total, but he managed to continue his offending by prioritizing a hitherto latent passion for nudity in public places. By the time of his death he had notched up more than six hundred convictions.

Paul Preston McCartney was born in Hartlepool. His parents were school teachers. He called his mother every week until her death, and afterwards he cooked for his father every Sunday, unless otherwise incarcerated. His older brother was a barrister and his younger sister a nurse. Paul tried several respectable jobs, but his criminal inclinations precluded lasting employment.

He once appeared on a reality television show which locked up the contestants in Alcatraz. The show was a commercial failure, and he hated every moment. But his appearance fee enabled him to fulfil a childhood dream and buy a Harley-Davidson. He was later convicted of failing to pay road tax.

\*\*\*

Trevor McDonald, who has died aged sixty-two, was a professor of medieval English at the University of Birmingham, best known for claiming to be a reincarnation of Santa Claus. For nearly fifteen years, he attended every lecture dressed as Father Christmas, and would holiday each winter in Lapland. Last year he was presented with the Reindeer Medal, the highest accolade of the Finnish Tourist Office.

Trevor Donald McDonald was born in Lima to a Scottish father and Peruvian mother. His father was an oil prospector, and Trevor spent most of his boyhood living on the edges of deserts and being instructed by local governesses in regional lore. It was the latter which prompted his mature mind to study medieval English language and literature as an undergraduate, and his enthusiasm was more than matched by his talent for innovative research. He wrote a number of influential academic essays, and one book on the history of medieval castles.

When forty years old, he was reluctantly persuaded by his son's primary school to dress up as Santa Claus at the Christmas fair. He collapsed unconscious and was taken to hospital. The doctors thought he had overheated in the costume. He later described it as a feeling of benign possession. Every Christmas from then on he handed out gifts, in costume, at local orphanages. His fame spread, and he was soon in demand nationally. His family were always supportive. 'He's doing good,' his now adult son once said, 'and I love him for that.'

\*\*\*

Margaret Drabble, who has died aged seventy-three, ran a knitwear empire that at its height could count

Prince Charles and Nelson Mandela among its customers. She had factories in some of the poorest countries in the world, and each factory was run as a refuge for women seeking to escape domestic violence. There were dormitories and allotments on site, and women who wanted to leave were encouraged to set up their own businesses with 'seedling' cash hand-outs. She was once nominated for the Nobel Peace Prize.

Herself the victim of a single-parent father prone to alcoholic rages, she ran away from home as a teenager with her younger sister. They took with them the only remaining possession of their mother, her sewing kit. They managed to survive, sleeping rough or in hostels, working as seamstresses, carrying out repairs for guests at local hotels. Their father's death the following year left them enough money to buy a flat with a shop downstairs. Margaret encouraged her sister's creativity for design, and soon the shop was flourishing.

Margaret Miranda Drabble was born in Church Aston. Her father was an unemployed miner. Her mother died during the birth of her younger sister. She was enrolled in the local comprehensive school, but often failed to attend for fear of revealing the bruises she suffered at her father's hands. She didn't marry, but she delighted in being an aunt, showering her nephews and niece with gifts and praise. She never once gave them a jumper.

\*\*\*

Edward Elgar, who has died aged sixty-three, was a traitor and celebrated communist. He was buried in Moscow with full military honours. The Russian President himself delivered the eulogy.

Edward Brian Elgar was born in Bristol. He was an engineer of precocious talent who, upon graduation, was approached for a job developing new weapons systems for the British military. He was lured by the promise of research funds and equipment to be put at the disposal of his maverick imagination. But at university he had fallen in love with a communist. Although the relationship did not last, it was enough to inspire a life-long commitment to the ideology, and secure an introduction to a communist spy-master. After several years with the

British military, Edward decided he was ready to leave for Russia.

Over a period of months, Edward developed a reputation for flatulence and poor personal hygiene. No guard wanted to stop him when one evening he waddled through the gate with ten roles of photographs stuffed down his trousers. That evening he was in Paris, and the next day Moscow. The Russian military were particularly interested in learning what they could about British military capability. But Edward also smuggled out plans for a new type of dam, coupled with blueprints of an experimental energy technology which he hoped would bring cheap electricity to the masses. He never knew what became of those blueprints.

In Russia, he turned his attentions to improving farming techniques. His work was so popular that a type of carrot is named after him.

*\*\*\**

Petula Clark, who has died aged ninety-seven, was a painter who painted over other people's work. Later hailed by Banksy as the originator of terrorist art, she only began her crusade of defacement after her retirement as a Post Office worker.

She was best known for having drawn a moustache in biro on a portrait of the Queen, and for using Dulux emulsion, her favourite medium, to paint anatomically detailed gonads on a sculpture by Henry Moore. He was her favourite artist, if number of modifications is any guide. Her only regret was having been outpaced by a French security guard to the Mona Lisa on her one visit to the Louvre. She was officially barred from the National Portrait Gallery, and every branch of the Tate. In her later years, she had to specialize in regional museums. When older and slower, she was invited to open the Museum of Modernism in Devon. At the ceremony, she was offered a blank wall to leave her mark, but turned it down. Unknown to her hosts, she had already defaced the women's toilets.

Petula Clark was born in Reigate. Her father was a milkman. Her mother taught art classes at the local primary school. Petula showed no more flare for art as a girl than she did as an adult, and left secondary school at sixteen with one O-level in

Scripture. She joined the Post Office that summer, and remained there until compulsory retirement. She was always coy about the motives for her artistic outrages. But she hated Picasso. She said he'd wrecked his own pictures already.

\*\*\*

Guy Fawkes, who has died aged sixty-seven, was best known as the rear end of a pantomime horse.

Guy was on a summer internship at BBC television studios when he was called upon by a panicking producer to fill in as the rear end of a pantomime horse on a children's show when the regular rear end phoned in sick. Guy kept the job for the next ten years. It was never clear what precise role the horse had on the show. It had no speaking lines, and mostly would wander around at the back of the set bumping into things. But it was popular with children, and the horse was often in demand to appear on stage or at charity events. Guy gave up the role when it became clear that he would never progress into television management as he had hoped.

Guy Martin Fawkes was born in Plymouth. After leaving children's entertainment, Guy returned home to join his mother working in the local bakery, before opening his own cake shop in Exeter.

The pantomime horse had no regular front end. On one occasion, the task was assigned to an unimpressed young woman, and Guy spent an uncomfortable half-hour with his hands on her behind. They later married.

***

Socrates, who has died aged fifty-four, slept rough on London's Embankment, except when in police custody for trying to steal the Crown Jewels from the Tower of London. By his own reckoning, he tried one hundred and seventeen times.

His name and life prior to the Embankment remained a mystery. His assaults on the Tower of London only began after nearly three years of sleeping rough. It was a wet winter morning, and he decided to 'try something stupid' for the chance of a dry police cell and a warm cup of tea. Wearing a bin liner as a cagoule, and with a baseball hat pulled down tight over his face, he managed to infiltrate the tail end of a Japanese tourist party as they entered the Tower. After several minutes of warming his hands with the air dryer in the toilets, he made his way to one of the less crowded display rooms. Borrowing a spear from a suit of armour, he charged at the glass casing, only to bounce back into the arms of a startled off-duty policeman.

Socrates became well known to the Chief Yeoman Warder. On his hundredth attempt, Socrates was presented with a Warder's Tudor bonnet. He wore it proudly every day to the soup kitchen until it was stolen from him one night while asleep. This made local news, and a group of celebrities offered in vain a reward for its safe return. Socrates kept cuttings of his exploits from newspapers he retrieved from rubbish bins, and these are now on display at the Visitor's Centre at the Tower.

***

David Beckham, who has died aged seventy-seven, was a gravedigger who enjoyed a brief moment of fame when an enterprising theatre producer cast him as a gravedigger in a new show he was then staging. This ploy attracted the attention of the media and secured an extended run for the show, about 14 days longer than its two weeks merited.

David St John Beckham was born in Nottingham. His father was a hospital porter. His younger brother, with whom he always enjoyed a close relationship, was the first British astronaut to walk in space. After leaving school, David earned his way with a number of casual jobs as a manual labourer at building sites and garden centres. He was happiest when working outdoors. Although envious of the views his brother's occupation provided, he pitied him the absence of weather. When the post of county gravedigger became available, David was first to apply. Although it did not pay as well as acting, he had more talent for it, and it offered secure employment in peaceful surroundings.

When not digging graves, he could be found leading tours of local cemeteries, or propping up the bar at his local pub, where he played 'a mean game of dominoes.' He and his brother once reached the World Finals in Jamaica as part of the team representing Britain. For convenience, David lived in rented rooms above the pub. He invented a pulley system, the most popular in use today, for lowering coffins into graves. He himself was cremated.

***

Vasco de Gama, who has died aged seventy-seven, was a magnificent charlatan so convincing that there were still some in high society prepared to defend his authenticity to the end. Vasco insisted he was the only living direct descendant of the last Pharaoh, a spectacular claim which saw him feted by the upper classes. Reportedly he never once bought a meal his whole life.

Vasco Ptolemy Arsinoe de Gama was born in Cairo. Supposedly, his father was a mystic philosopher and his mother a priestess. Both died before Vasco arrived in Europe. He disembarked a cruise liner with a procession of servants carrying trunks containing one of the most important collections of Egyptian artefacts ever seen in the West, second only to the treasure trove of Tutankhamun's tomb. He claimed the artefacts were household wares from his city *riad*. He was off-hand in donating them to the British Museum. Apparently he had far more important pieces in his palace on the edge of the city. That claim was never confirmed, and he never returned to Egypt.

He was especially welcome at Buckingham Palace, where he once sought to bestow upon the Queen the title of Grand High Empress of Luxor, along with a gold tiara inlaid with silver in the shape of the eye of Isis. She wore it the following year to Ascot, when her horse, Mespots Fancy, came home at 7-1.

***

Fred Astaire, who has died aged seventy-nine, was a prison officer who later became personal assistant to a notorious criminal.

Peter Andre was convicted for his part in hijacking a security van containing three million pounds in diamonds. It was almost four weeks before an anonymous tip-off pointed the police to a third-floor flat in Peckham. It turned out to be booby-trapped. When the police entered, bombs were detonated, and the dust settled to reveal the bodies of two officers and three gang members. The only surviving gang member was Andre, who had been visiting his mother in hospital that day. He was arrested one week later while attending her funeral.

There was a persistent but unproven rumour that Andre had killed his accomplices before setting the bombs and calling the police. He was convicted only of robbery. The diamonds were never recovered.

Andre was sent to Wormwood Scrubs, where Fred was a prison officer. Andre had a magnetic personality, and Fred was uncritically loyal to a person whose determination and assurance he admired. When Andre was released after twelve years, Fred resigned his post to become Andre's personal assistant. His first task was to accompany Andre to a casino where, to the astonishment of those at the table, Andre won a sum of money conveniently described as three million pounds less twenty per cent commission.

Fred Ballantine Astaire was born in Barrow. He became a prison officer to be closer to his father, a decorator and regular inmate with a string of convictions for petty theft from the houses he painted.

*\*\**

Horatio Nelson, who has died aged sixty-nine, was a mathematician who created a problem which has yet to be solved. He also spent many years of his adult life in the Himalayas attempting to prove the existence of the Yeti he claimed to have seen as a child.

Horatio Peter Nelson was born in Bristol. His father was a diplomat, and one posting saw the family move to Nepal. Rupert was then a teenager with an interest for trekking. A holiday expedition saw him and a school friend camping alone on Annapurna. Needing to relieve himself one night, Horatio stepped outside the tent to be confronted in the moonlight by 'a creature the size of an orang-utan, with the dappled fur of a snow leopard.' The creature startled, and by the time Horatio had roused his friend, the Yeti had vanished. The morning revealed footprints around the camp, but the boys' photographs were dismissed by zoologists as a hoax.

Horatio read mathematics at university, and chose a career as a secondary school teacher. During his tenure as head of department at Kingston Grammar School, he devised a problem for homework which crossed Pythagoras' theorem with

Euclid's, only to find that he couldn't produce a solution. He published the problem on-line to great interest, but no answer has yet been found.

Horatio spent most summers in Nepal, volunteering as a mathematics teacher in mountain schools, and trekking several hours each night in search of the Yeti. He never came across it again. But he did discover a new orchid, which bears the name of his understanding wife.

\*\*\*

Johnny Cash, who has died aged eighty-three, was the lead singer in a little-known punk rock band, who made a fortune he didn't need by writing a Christmas number one.

Johnathan Simon de Montfort Cavanagh was born in Chelsea. His father owned the private bank synonymous with the family name. His mother was independently wealthy as an antiques dealer. Johnny went to Eton, which he described as 'the best years of my life.' This was reflected in atrocious A-level results and the end of his education. He liked to style himself an anarchist, and adopted the name 'Cash' to mock the rich, or to mock himself, or both – his ideology was never as well defined as his dress sense. He 'squatted' in a comfortable flat in Fulham owned by a shadowy off-shore corporation who never seemed to worry. He was unpopular with neighbours for his raucous parties, attended by fashionable revolutionaries and press photographers. Each would begin with Johnny's band playing their latest diatribe.

'I can't sing, but I can shout,' he once accurately explained.

In a shock moment of musicality, he once discovered that he'd written a Christmas song. A family friend in the music business, who repeatedly refused to sign Johnny and his punk band, was as surprised as anyone to discern the song's potential. It was recorded by a teenage star of reality television. It landed the Christmas number one and guaranteed annual royalties. The singer subsequently sank into obscurity and alcoholism.

Johnny was also a regular writer for Mills & Boon, and attended church every Sunday.

## THE MONK'S TALE

### Stories about Happiness

A collection of fables, readings and meditations which recount the experiences of a monk as he seeks to understand life and happiness.

(Available November 2014)

*Excerpts*...

The abbot and the monk were returning from town.

A few drops of summer rain fell fat on the abbot's head. He wiped his brow with a sleeve and set off at a canter. The rain began to fall straight and heavy, so the monk took up the chase. The water in the street ran in streams. The monk sloshed his way through with sodden feet and gritted teeth. The rain came down in torrents. The world was formless and translucent grey. The monk scowled. The clothes clung to his chest with a wet chill. By the time he reached the porch at the temple gate, his jaw ached and his fists were clenched. The abbot was waiting. He too was drenched from head to toe as if the gods themselves had dunked him in a tea cup.

'I am wet,' said the abbot. 'But you are wet and angry.'

\*\*\*

The rainstorm continued to batter the roof. The monk trudged down the corridor. His head drooped. The water trickled off his nose and dripped down his sleeves. His feet were slippery on the wooden floorboards. He left a trail of pools and puddles that shimmered in the twilight of darkened skies. They would need mopping up or the varnish might peel.

He wrung out his clothes in the bathroom and pulled on some robes which were dry and comforting. He'd seen the clouds gathering on his way into town. Why hadn't he borrowed an umbrella? What a fool! He returned to the corridor with a knotted brow and an old towel. It took an hour of self-criticism to clean up the mess. By the end of it, he still hadn't borrowed the umbrella.

# LITTLE IDEA

## Learning Kung Fu in Hong Kong

The story of the author's obsessive attempts to master kung fu while living in Hong Kong. The search for perfection takes in a range of other disciplines, from mindfulness through the Alexander Technique to fasting Marathon Monks. Told with humour, this book gives an authentic flavour of Hong Kong and its everyday kung fu grandmasters.

(Available January 2015)

# Chapter One

I was 34 years old, a university law lecturer and father of three. But I was living in Hong Kong, and I wanted to learn kung fu.

I first got the taste for martial arts as a foreign exchange student at university in the Netherlands. I was looking for something new to try, and the only exercise offered at the university centre compatible with my timetable was the Japanese martial art of aikido. So one day I walked into class. The teacher spoke no English. My Dutch was even worse. Yet despite the language barrier, the teacher was inspirational. He moved with grace. His techniques were flowing. He exuded a spirit of passionate commitment and kindly patience. In his qualities, he was the very embodiment of *budo*, the martial way. In his appearance, he had glaring eyes and terrible teeth. I was a diligent student. I turned up to every class. Sitting on the rubber mats, I watched his footwork intently. I watched his hands keenly. For some reason, I couldn't watch both his footwork and his hands; it had to be one or the other. So my progress was slow, but I was full of enthusiasm. Each class lasted two hours, and I finished soaked with sweat, panting for breath and gasping for water, bruised and exhausted and elated.

When my exchange programme ended, I returned to university in England and sought out my local aikido club. Over the following year, I was lucky enough to train with some outstanding practitioners, including the Master of the Way, as the most senior grandmaster is titled. He moved with a light rustle of clothes, and his technique was softly persuasive. But my local club was turgid. The class was slow. No-one was fired up. Some of the students seemed irritated to be there, and released their frustration on their training partners. I was increasingly battered and increasingly bitter. But there was another club which trained at the university gym at the same time. That class was more popular. It was active and noisy. Everyone seemed to be having more fun. And they wore black uniforms. It was the Korean martial art of sulkido.

For four years, I trained daily in sulkido. The syllabus was an all-encompassing amalgamation of various styles of traditional Korean martial arts. There were hard forms, which are solo patterns of movement performed in a muscular staccato rhythm. There were soft forms, where the movements flow one into the next in a circular, seamless manner. There were hand techniques, which are hundreds of different joint locks and throws, collected together into various groups, depending on whether you use one hand or two, and whether you were grabbed by the wrist or the clothes, from the front or the back, and so on. The hand techniques were liberally sprinkled with the use of pressure points. These are vulnerable points on the body which cannot be concealed by building muscle. The application of intense pressure in the right place can produce debilitating pain that lasts long after the victim has stopped swearing at their training partner.

And there was more. There were break-falls, teaching how to fall over in the least damaging way. There were punches. There were breathing techniques. And there were kicks. Lots of kicks: kicks with the front leg and kicks with the back leg; standing kicks and stepping kicks and jumping kicks; spinning kicks and turning kicks and jumping-and-spinning kicks. These did not come naturally to me. But after hundreds of hours of repetitive practice, they were adequate. And the rest of the syllabus I could do well. I was awarded my black belt.

And so things continued. I graduated from university and acquired a job, still training in sulkido every day. Occasionally I would accessorize with techniques pilfered from other styles of martial arts.

But then I had children. And my first children were twins.

There was a programme on television about what could turn ordinary people into murderers. Apparently, the answer is new-born twins. The presenter, a former politician, but a well-educated and rounded liberal nevertheless, was exploring the psychology of murder. He subjected himself to an experiment whereby the scientists, or whoever they were, sought to prove just how quickly his own temperament could be changed, given the right stimuli. So he was given a regular job, nine to five with a sandwich break for lunch, and then home to new-born twins, played by programmed dolls. They would cry every time they needed changing or feeding or attention of any kind. Exhausted, sleep-deprived, probably under-nourished, and faced with something he couldn't reason with, the politician soon became paranoid and aggressive and borderline murderous. It only took three days.

My reaction to twins was different, of course, because they were my children. So it included wonder, fear, responsibility, and love, as well as exhaustion, sleep-deprivation, malnourishment, and maddening frustration. But the aggression was there. Only it wasn't directed towards my own family. It was directed towards the rest of the world. I was in a heightened and perpetual state of paranoia. In my mind, other people posed a threat. Some posed a physical threat. Others posed a threat to the financial security or emotional stability of my family, in various subtle and pernicious ways. My response was one of covert physical aggression.

For example, I would be out for an afternoon walk, pushing the buggy down a narrow street in the fading winter light, when another pedestrian would appear further along the pavement. Before they were fifty metres from me, I had already pictured a number of possible confrontations, all of them ending with the other's death, and me running away with the buggy before the police could arrive. The pedestrian might turn out to be a young man or an old granny. But you never knew, not even with old grannies. The only way to be certain was death. I had three favourite ways of killing people. This was not healthy.

Despite my passion for martial arts, I gave it up, more fearful of what I was becoming. I took up yoga. The yoga teacher was pushy. It made me want to hit her. So I gave up yoga too, and decided to weather the storm as best I could on a pacifist diet that precluded all television with even a hint of violence, and that meant pretty much anything I ever watched. Eventually we got rid of the television.

And that was the way it was until we arrived in Hong Kong. My children, now three of them, were a little older, and sleeping through the night, though never the same night. We had taken the job in Hong Kong for the adventure of it, so mentally I was feeling refreshed. I was running regularly, and so fit, despite Hong Kong's literally fatal air pollution. And in public spaces everywhere, morning and evening, people were practising martial arts. There was tai chi and fan dancing and sword play and lion dancing and kung fu. Some of them were terrible. Some of them were great masters. They wore stained and tattered t-shirts. They wore trousers with sparkles down the side. There were children as young as three, and women who had begun to practise in their late seventies. They hid behind trees in the park, or preened at their reflections in the windows of the public library. There were serious faces and jolly laughter. There was dedication and playfulness. All around there was clamour and movement and energy. The excitement was building. I couldn't watch without wanting to join in. There was only one question now: which would I choose?

# MONKEY KING

## The legend reimagined

In the middle of an ocean was an island, and in the middle of the island was a mountain.

The ocean was a deep blue which glinted in the midday sun. The island hung with lush jungle and bright flowers. The mountain rose tall above the forests and high into the clouds.

At the top of the mountain was a rock. The winds blew about the rock, whispering messages from afar. They shaped it into a stone egg, warmed by Heaven and nourished by Earth.

A storm gathered about the mountain. The ocean grew turbulent and blackened. The island trees thrashed. The mountain was thrown into brooding shadow as the clouds loomed thick and restless. A clap of thunder shook the sky, and a purple neon flash of lightning cleaved the egg in two. There was Monkey.

\*\*\*

Join Monkey as his journey progresses from incorrigible tormenter through heroic adventurer to wise teacher in this reimagining of the Chinese classic.

(Available March 2015)

Printed in Great Britain
by Amazon.co.uk, Ltd.,
Marston Gate.